KNOW YOUR IDENTITY

PAUL HAMPTON

Copyright © 2022 by Paul Hampton. 845860

All rights reserved. No part of this book may be reproduced or transmitted in any form or by any means, electronic or mechanical, including photocopying, recording, or by any information storage and retrieval system, without permission in writing from the copyright owner.

This is a work of fiction. Names, characters, places and incidents either are the product of the author's imagination or are used fictitiously, and any resemblance to any actual persons, living or dead, events, or locales is entirely coincidental.

To order additional copies of this book, contact:
Xlibris
844-714-8691
www.Xlibris.com
Orders@Xlibris.com

ISBN:	Softcover	978-1-6698-4246-0
	EBook	978-1-6698-4245-3

Print information available on the last page

Rev. date: 09/15/2022

Know Your Identity

When Christian woke up and opened his eyes one morning, it was so bright that it made him want to immediately close them again.

Instead of lying there and having a bad attitude, he told himself,“If I get up, get dressed, brush my teeth, and make my bed before going downstairs for breakfast, it will make Mom and Dad so proud!” So that’s exactly what he did.

Cereal

When he sat down to eat his cereal and toast with his parents and little sister, his mom looked at him and smiled. “Good morning, honey! I see you got dressed; did you remember to brush your teeth before you came down?”

“I sure did, and I even made my bed!” Christian answered with excitement. At this, both his mom and dad and even his little sister looked shocked.

“Well, I must say, I’m impressed, son. Good job! Way to take initiative. You are very responsible,” his dad told him proudly.

As Christian sat there feeling great about himself and the day ahead, he quickly realized he was going to be late for the school bus. “Got to go–I’m already late!” he said. Then he grabbed his lunch and sprinted out the door.

When he stepped on the bus, he was feeling a little embarrassed. He was almost never late, and he hated the thought of the whole bus having to wait on him. He was about to sit in one of the back seats when a kid that Christian recognized but didn't really talk to shouted out, "Way to go, loser! Now we are all going to be late." Now Christian was even more embarrassed; after a great start to the day, it seemed like the day was going downhill.

Once he got to school and class started, everything seemed to go normal. No one made fun of him again, and the teacher never called out his name to read from the textbook. At lunch he ate with his friends at their favorite lunch table. Christian told some funny jokes, and everyone was laughing and having a great lunch. “You are so funny,” one of his friends said. Suddenly, Christian felt confident again; maybe, just maybe, the day was going well after all.

10

At recess, Christian and some of his friends were playing a game of basketball. His team was down by one basket, and Christian had the ball with a chance to win the game. When he threw the ball up, he really thought it was going to go in, but it bounced off the rim and didn't go in.

"Ha, I knew you would miss; you stink at basketball!" one of the kids on the other team said. Now Christian was feeling sad and guilty, as if he had let his friends down. Now he was certain that this day was no good, and neither was he!

Later that evening, as Christian sat at dinner with his parents and sister, his mom asked him about his day. “How was your day, hon? How are you feeling?”

“I don’t know,” Christian mumbled. “Kind of good and kind of bad.”

“Oh, really? Why good and bad?” his mom replied.

“Well, this morning, I felt good–like I made you and Dad proud. But then I was late for the bus, and I made all my friends wait on me. I was feeling pretty guilty and sad. But then at lunch, I made everyone laugh and all my friends told me I was really funny, so I felt good again, as if I was popular. Then at recess I missed the game-winning shot during our basketball game, and the other team teased me. So I felt sad again, as if I was no good.”

“Wow,” his mom said, “that’s a lot. I’m glad you told me all of that. I’ve got an idea; follow me.” Then she headed for the living room.

Holy
Bible

Christian followed his mom as she grabbed her Bible. She turned to 1 Peter 2:9–10, where it says that we are a chosen people, God's very own possession. And it also says that our identity is God's own people.

Suddenly Christian realized that it was important to be responsible, make your bed, get dressed, and brush your teeth, but those things don't decide who you are. And of course you want to be on time and not make people wait on you, but those things don't decide who you are. It's great to make people laugh and spread joy, and you should always want to do your best at everything you do. But those things don't decide who you are. What decides who you are is the Word of God. It says you are a chosen child of God, and *that* is your identity!

Printed in the United States
by Baker & Taylor Publisher Services